OCEAN

HARBOR

LITTLE
TOOT

LITTLE TOOT

PICTURES and STORY
by
HARDIE GRAMATKY

G.P. PUTNAM'S SONS

G. P. PUTNAM'S SONS
A division of Penguin Young Readers Group.
Published by The Penguin Group.
Penguin Group (USA) Inc., 375 Hudson Street, New York, NY 10014, U.S.A.
Penguin Group (Canada), 90 Eglinton Avenue East, Suite 700, Toronto, Ontario, Canada M4P 2Y3
(a division of Pearson Penguin Canada Inc.).
Penguin Books Ltd, 80 Strand, London WC2R 0RL, England.
Penguin Ireland, 25 St. Stephen's Green, Dublin 2, Ireland (a division of Penguin Books Ltd.).
Penguin Group (Australia), 250 Camberwell Road, Camberwell, Victoria 3124, Australia
(a division of Pearson Australia Group Pty Ltd).
Penguin Books India Pvt Ltd, 11 Community Centre, Panchsheel Park, New Delhi - 110 017, India.
Penguin Group (NZ), 67 Apollo Drive, Mairangi Bay, Auckland 1311, New Zealand
(a division of Pearson New Zealand Ltd).
Penguin Books (South Africa) (Pty) Ltd, 24 Sturdee Avenue, Rosebank, Johannesburg 2196, South Africa.
Penguin Books Ltd, Registered Offices: 80 Strand, London WC2R 0RL, England.

Printed in the USA
Design by Katrina Damkoehler. Text set in Caslon Book.

Library of Congress Cataloging-in-Publication Data
Gramatky, Hardie. 1907-1979 Little Toot.
Summary: Little Toot, the tugboat, conquers his fear of rough seas
when he singlehandedly rescues an ocean liner during a storm.
[1. Tugboat–Fiction.] I. Title. PZ7.G7654Li 1978
[E] 78-4801

ISBN 978-0-399-24713-2
3 5 7 9 10 8 6 4 2

A NOTE TO THE READER

As Hardie Gramatky's only child, I was so blessed to have an optimistic, humble, loving dad–a person who welcomed children and their parents to visit his studio, who was always delighted to hear that someone loved *Little Toot* and his other books, and who joyfully painted until the end of his life at age 72.

Over the years since his death in 1979, I have seen new editions of *Little Toot* come out and have witnessed renewed interest in his fine art watercolors (Andrew Wyeth called him one of "the twenty great American watercolorists"). However, each time I looked at his classic children's book *Little Toot*, in print since 1939, I noticed that his wonderfully vibrant red and blue colors had faded to insipid oranges and grays over years of printings. One day when my husband, Kendall, and I were visiting Putnam to talk about what would have been Dad's 100th birthday on April 12, 2007, I brought a first edition with us. We all marveled over the freshness of the original colors and talked about how we could bring back the vibrancy in a "restored classic edition." The book you are holding in your hands was created with some color sketches from Dad's original manuscript, some original artwork given to the New York Public Library (including endpapers that haven't been seen for forty years!) and scans made from that first edition.

My wish is that you will read this edition with fresh eyes and an open heart and that Dad and Mom are looking down with great joy knowing that *Little Toot* is still a mischievous, imaginative tugboat that children love.

Linda Gramatky Smith

At the foot of an old, old wharf lives the cutest, silliest little tugboat you ever saw. A *very* handsome tugboat with a brand-new candy-stick smokestack.

His name is Little Toot. And this name he came by through no fault of his own. Blow hard as he would, the only sound that came out of his whistle was a gay, small toot-toot-toot.

But what he couldn't create in sound, Little Toot made up for in smoke. From his chubby smokestack he would send up a volley of smoke balls which bubbled over his wake like balloons. Hence, when he got all "steamed up," Little Toot used to feel very important . . .

Then the flag at his masthead would dance like the tail of a puppy dog when he's happy . . .

And he flaunted his signals like a man-o'-war.

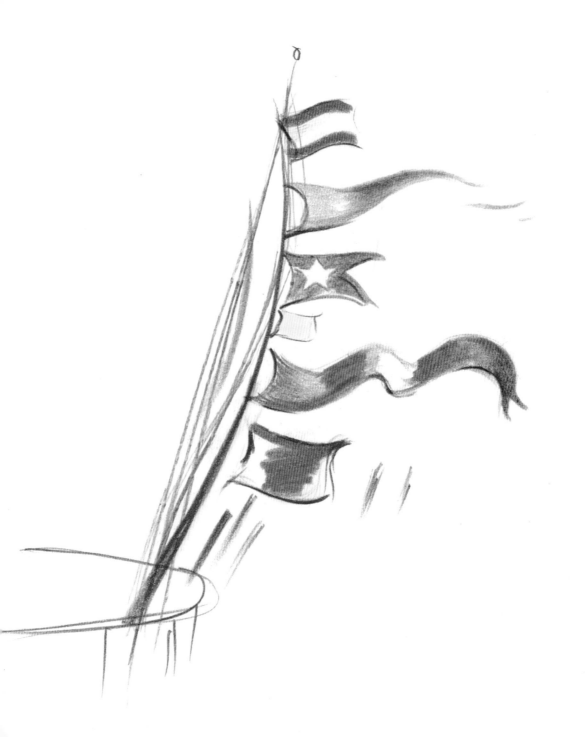

Now, the river where Little Toot lives is full of ships. They come from ports all over the world, bringing crews who speak strange tongues, and bringing even stranger cargoes—hides from Buenos Aires, copra from the South Seas, whale oil from the Antarctic, and fragrant teas from distant Asia. So there is always work for tugboats to do, either pushing ships into the docks to be unloaded, or else pulling them into the stream and down the channel to the ocean to begin a new voyage.

So a tugboat's life is a busy, exciting one, and Little Toot was properly right in the middle of it. His father, Big Toot, is the biggest and fastest tugboat on the river. Why, Big Toot can make *more* smoke and kick up *more* water than any two of the other boats put together.

As for Grandfather Toot, he is an old sea dog who breathes smoke . . . and tells of his mighty deeds on the river.

You'd think that Little Toot, belonging to such an important family, would have his mind on work. But no. Little Toot hated work. He saw no sense in pulling ships fifty times bigger than himself all the way down to the ocean. And he was scared of the wild seas that lay in wait outside the channel, beyond where the harbor empties into the ocean.

Little Toot had no desire to be tossed around. He preferred the calm water of the river itself, where he could always find plenty of fun. Like gliding, for example . . .

Or playing thread-the-needle around the piers.

Or, what was even fancier, cutting figure 8's . . .

Little Toot liked nothing better than to make a really fine figure 8. First you throw your weight on one side, then on the other. And the result never failed to delight him, although his antics annoyed the hard-working tugboats awfully.

But he kept on making figure 8's that grew bigger and bigger until one day, carried away by the joy of it all, he made one so big it took up the whole river. Indeed, there was hardly room for it between the two shores . . .

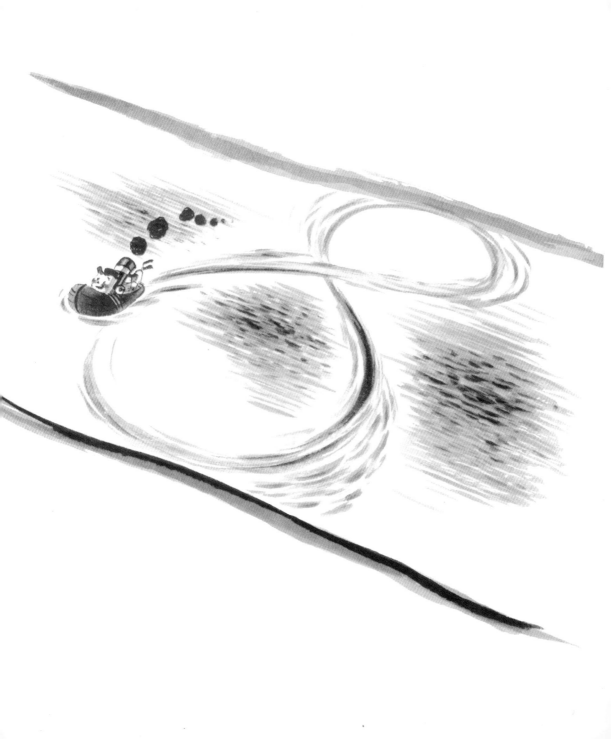

And no room at all for a big tug named J. G. McGillicuddy, which was bound downstream to pick up a string of coal barges from Hoboken. J. G. McGillicuddy had little love for other tugboats, anyway, and a frivolous one like Little Toot made him mad. As witness . . .

This by itself was bad enough; but, unfortunately
for Little Toot, the other tugboats had seen what
had happened. So they began to make fun of him,
calling him a sissy who only knew how to play . . .

Poor Little Toot. He was ashamed and angry, but
there was nothing he could do about it except blow
those silly smoke balls . . .

But the more he blew, the more the other boats laughed at him.

Little Toot couldn't stand it. He fled to his favorite hiding place alongside the wharf, where his taunting friends could not reach him; and there he just sat and sulked.

After he had moped a while Little
Toot saw, headed down the river, a
great ocean liner.

And pulling it were four tugboats, with his own father Big Toot right up in front.

The sight of that brave, bustling work made Little Toot think. He thought harder than ever in his life, and then—all of a sudden—a great idea burst over him. He *wouldn't* be a silly, frivolous little tugboat any more. He would work like the best of them. After all, wasn't he the son of Big Toot, the mightiest tug on the river? Well, he would make Big Toot proud of him. He'd show them all! Full of ambition, he started eagerly downstream.

He sidled hopefully up to one big ship after another, tooting for them to heave a towline. But they supposed he was still only a nuisance, and would have nothing to do with him. Oscar, the Scandinavian, rudely blew steam in his face . . .

And the others were too busy with their own affairs to notice a bothersome little tug. They knew him too well!

But the rudest of all was a great transatlantic liner which blasted him right out of the water.

That was too much for Little Toot. He wasn't wanted anywhere or by anyone. With his spirits drooping he let the tide carry him where it willed. He was so *lonesome* . . .

Floating aimlessly downstream he grew sadder and sadder until he was utterly miserable. He was sunk so deep in his own despair he didn't even notice that the sky had grown dark and that the wind was whipping up into a real storm.

Suddenly he heard a sound that was like no sound he had ever heard before–

It was the *Ocean*. The Great Ocean that Little Toot had never seen. And the noise came from the waves as they dashed and pounded against the rocks.

But that wasn't all.
Against the black sky climbed a . . .

. . . brilliant, flaming rocket.

When Little Toot looked hard, he saw, jammed between two huge rocks, an ocean liner which his father had towed many times up and down the river.

It was truly a terrible thing to see . . .

Little Toot went wild with excitement! He began puffing those silly balls of smoke out of his smokestack . . .

And as he did, a wonderful thought struck him. Why, those smoke balls could probably be seen 'way up the river, where his father and grandfather were. So he puffed a signal, thus . . .

'Way up the river they saw it . . .

Of course they had no idea who was making the
signals, but they knew it meant "come quickly." So
they all dropped what they were doing to race to
the rescue.

Out from many wharves steamed
a great fleet–
    big boats,
        little boats,
            fat ones,
        and skinny ones . . .

. . . With Big Toot himself right in the lead, like an admiral at the head of his fleet . . .

Just in time, too, because Little Toot, still puffing out his S.O.S., was hard put to it to stay afloat.

One wave spun him around till he was dizzy; and another tossed him up so high he was glad when a spiral-shaped wave came along for him to glide down on . . .

Before he could spit the salt water out of his smokestack, still another wave came along and tossed him up again . . .

It looked as though he'd never get down.

All this was pretty awful for a tugboat that was used to the smooth water of the river. What made it terrifying was the fact that out of the corner of his eye, when he was thus hung on a wave, Little Toot saw that the fleet wasn't able to make headway against such fierce seas.

Even Grandfather Toot was bellowing
he has never seen such a storm.

Little Toot was scared green . . .

Something had to be done. But all that Little Toot had ever learned to do was blow out those silly smoke balls.

Where he was, the channel was like a narrow bottle neck with the whole ocean trying to pour in at once.

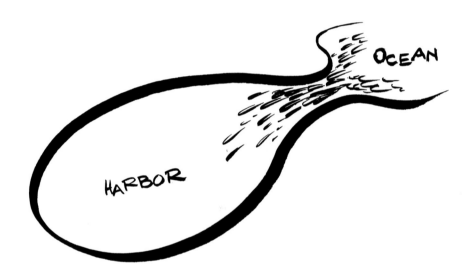

That was why the fleet couldn't make any headway. The force of the seas simply swept them back . . .

Indeed, they were on the verge of giving up entirely when suddenly above the storm they heard a gay, familiar toot . . .

It was Little Toot. Not wasting his strength butting the waves as they had done. But bouncing from crest to crest, like a rubber ball. The pounding hurt like everything, but Little Toot kept right on going.

And when Big Toot looked out to sea through his binoculars, he saw the crew on the great vessel throw a line to Little Toot.

It was a wonderful thing to see. When the line was made fast, Little Toot waited for a long moment . . .

And then, when a huge wave swept under the liner, lifting it clear of the rocks, he pulled with all of his might. *The liner came free!*

The people on board began to cheer . . .

And the whole tugboat fleet insisted upon Little
Toot's escorting the great boat back into the harbor.

Little Toot was a hero! And Grand-father Toot blasted the news all over the river.

Well, after that Little Toot became quite a different fellow. He even changed his tune . . .

And it is said that he can haul as
big a load as his father can . . .

. . . that is, when Big Toot hasn't a
very big load to haul . . .

HARDIE GRAMATKY (1907–1979) was born in Dallas and grew up in California. He began his art career as an animator for Walt Disney and helped start the California watercolor movement. He then moved to the East Coast to set up his own art studio, doing advertising and magazine illustration. From his studio, he had a bird's-eye view of vessels passing on the East River in New York. He was intrigued by the Moran tugboats, which were his inspiration for writing *Little Toot*. He wrote and illustrated fourteen children's books and won over eighty prizes as a fine artist.